# ON THE TRAIL OF

# Sacagawea

## PETER LOURIE

BOYDS MILLS PRESS

# Also by Peter Lourie

*Amazon*

*Hudson River*

*Yukon River*

*Erie Canal*

*Everglades*

*Rio Grande*

*Mississippi River*

*Lost Treasure of the Inca*

*The Lost Treasure of Captain Kidd: A Novel*

To my children
—P. L.

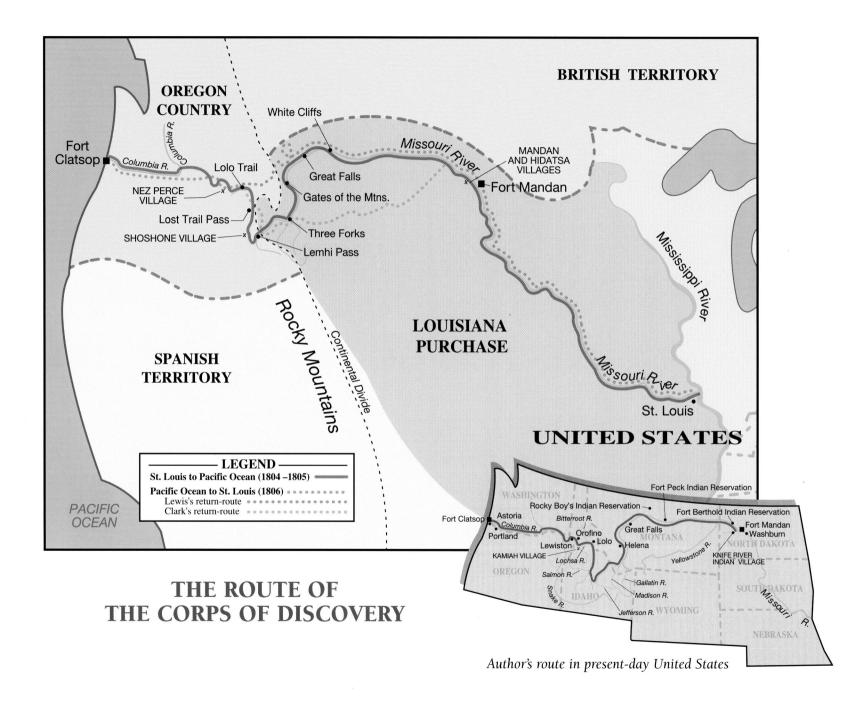

**BRITISH TERRITORY**

**OREGON COUNTRY**

White Cliffs

*Columbia R.*

Fort Clatsop

*Columbia R.*

Lolo Trail

Great Falls

NEZ PERCE VILLAGE

Gates of the Mtns.

Lost Trail Pass

SHOSHONE VILLAGE

Three Forks

Lemhi Pass

*Missouri River*

MANDAN AND HIDATSA VILLAGES

Fort Mandan

*Mississippi River*

**SPANISH TERRITORY**

Rocky Mountains

Continental Divide

**LOUISIANA PURCHASE**

*Missouri River*

St. Louis

**UNITED STATES**

**LEGEND**
St. Louis to Pacific Ocean (1804–1805)
Pacific Ocean to St. Louis (1806)
Lewis's return-route
Clark's return-route

*PACIFIC OCEAN*

**THE ROUTE OF THE CORPS OF DISCOVERY**

Fort Peck Indian Reservation

WASHINGTON

Rocky Boy's Indian Reservation

Fort Berthold Indian Reservation

Fort Clatsop

Astoria

*Columbia R.*

*Bitterroot R.*

Portland

Orofino

Lolo

Great Falls

Fort Mandan

Washburn

Lewiston

MONTANA

Helena

NORTH DAKOTA

KAMIAH VILLAGE

*Lochsa R.*

*Yellowstone R.*

KNIFE RIVER INDIAN VILLAGE

OREGON

*Salmon R.*

*Gallatin R.*

SOUTH DAKOTA

*Snake R.*

IDAHO

*Madison R.*

*Missouri R.*

*Jefferson R.*

WYOMING

NEBRASKA

*Author's route in present-day United States*

# Contents

# Prologue

*William Clark*

*Sacagawea and son*

*Meriwether Lewis*

**N**early two hundred years ago, before the days of railroads, before most settlers knew what lay west of the Mississippi, Captains Meriwether Lewis and William Clark ventured into lands known only to native peoples. They were commissioned by President Thomas Jefferson to explore the Missouri River to its source and find a direct and practical water route to the Pacific Ocean. Along the way, they were also expected to record what they saw: the geography, the people, the animals, and the plants.

In the spring of 1804, Lewis and Clark set off up the Missouri River with forty-five adventurers who called themselves the Corps of Discovery. It was the first organized expedition of the United States government to explore the West. They got as far as present-day Washburn, North Dakota, some 1,500 miles upriver from St. Louis, when winter set in. They built a small fort named Fort Mandan near the Knife River, a tributary of the Missouri, and endured a long Northern Plains winter with the Mandan and Hidatsa Indians.

Temperatures finally began to rise at the end of March, and a few buffalo fell through the river ice. The corps made preparations to head west into uncharted territory. Before they left Fort Mandan, however, they

*Ready to follow the trail*

hired a French interpreter, Toussaint Charbonneau, who spoke fluent Hidatsa. Many people believe today that Charbonneau was hired because he planned to bring his sixteen-year-old Shoshone wife, Sacagawea, whose name means "Bird Woman" in the Hidatsa language. The captains thought she might help in negotiations for horses with the Shoshone, who lived faraway in the Rocky Mountains, where she had been captured by a Hidatsa raiding party as a little girl.

A few months before leaving Fort Mandan, Sacagawea had given birth to a child she named Jean Baptiste. On April 7, 1805, Sacagawea strapped her newborn baby boy on her back and set off with the Corps of Discovery on one of the greatest journeys ever undertaken in the history of the United States.

My family wanted to learn more about the young Indian girl who had been so instrumental in the success of this monumental voyage. We wanted to compare what we would see today to what Sacagawea saw nearly two hundred years ago. We especially wanted to hear the Indian point of view both on Sacagawea herself and on the Lewis and Clark Expedition. For it was this expedition, more than any subsequent one, that opened the West. In order to follow in Sacagawea's footsteps, my wife, Melissa, and I, along with our children, Suzanna and Walker, rented a van. We lifted a canoe and two kayaks onto the roof. We packed camping equipment and books. Like a little Corps of Discovery, we were ready to follow Sacagawea's trail to the Pacific Ocean.

# Part One

## Fort Mandan

We began our journey in early July and headed to the confluence of the Missouri and Knife Rivers in North Dakota, where the corps had built Fort Mandan. Here Lewis and Clark met Sacagawea and learned of her Shoshone background.

For five months at the fort, the corps prepared for their journey west. To learn what they might find, they questioned British-Canadian fur trappers and Hidatsa men, who knew the area from long hunting and raiding trips. We visited the reconstructed fort, a triangular-shaped structure with two rows of rooms, each about fourteen feet square. Today's Fort Mandan, although not in the exact place as the original, looks much as it would have in 1804.

When the Corps of Discovery had arrived in the area, they found an actual city of native peoples. The Mandan and Hidatsa lived in five villages of great earth lodges along the Missouri and Knife Rivers. Craterlike depressions where the lodges once stood are still visible today. The villages were surrounded by ditches and embankments of clay. Lewis and Clark estimated about 4,400 people were living in the area. This was a center for trading because of nearby deposits of Knife River flint, one of the best flints for making stone tools on the Northern Plains. Many of today's Mandan and Hidatsa, however, live miles away on the Fort Berthold Reservation, and the Knife River seemed unusually silent when we canoed up the little stream.

Our first night along the Missouri we slept in a tepee not far from the original site of the fort, which is now

*Fort Mandan, reconstructed*

*These circular depressions are evidence of the earth lodges that once stood on the banks of the Knife River.*

underwater. We were guests of a North Dakota couple who run canoe trips along the Missouri. My children played in their kayaks, tipped them over, and swam in the river like seals. When we retired for the night, we lit a fire in the tepee, which made it very smoky inside but kept the mosquitoes away.

## Fort Berthold Reservation

The next day we drove to the Fort Berthold Reservation where the Hidatsa, Mandan, and another tribe, the Arikara, all live together. Marilyn Hudson, a very helpful woman of Hidatsa descent, took us to see the community gardens. We watched the children on the reservation work with hoes. Suzanna and Walker were asked to help out.

Marilyn explained that the Fort Berthold Reservation is making efforts to reintroduce native seeds and traditional gardening techniques. Eventually, the children will plant and harvest Mandan corn, Hidatsa beans, and other native vegetables. But the land they till today is different from what Sacagawea may have seen.

Over the past fifty years, the Missouri River has changed. In the Dakotas and much of Montana, it no longer flows freely. Dams have been built for hydroelectric power, for irrigation, and for flood control. Huge reservoirs have been formed behind these dams, flooding the surrounding terrain. When the Garrison Dam was built and formed the 178-mile-long Lake

*A Mandan earth lodge photographed in 1908*

Sakakawea, the Mandan and Hidatsa lost much of their agricultural land. So it was wonderful to see the children of the tribes growing beans and corn again. We also learned that many here still speak Hidatsa. Although there are only a handful of Mandan speakers left, that language, too, is being preserved. The young are taking a renewed interest in the ancient traditions of the tribe.

We left the reservation and passed on through the North Unit of Theodore Roosevelt National Park, where we found prairie dogs. Lewis and Clark called them "barking squirrels." Beyond the prairie dog village, fifteen bison lounged in the heat of the afternoon. I tried to imagine what it must have been like in Sacagawea's day, when an estimated sixty million bison roamed the plains.

*The Fort Berthold Reservation: Children plant vegetables in the community gardens.*

13

*This photograph of the Assiniboin chief Wets It was taken nearly one hundred years after Lewis tried to meet Chief Rosebud.*

*Ken Ryan of the Assiniboin tribe was tribal chairman from 1984 to 1987.*

## Fort Peck Reservation

Melissa took the wheel of the van, and our own little corps headed west. We read passages from the journals that Lewis and Clark each kept as they followed the Missouri to its source. One thing that surprised me was the lack of contact they made with tribes along their route. The captains had heard tales about the "war-like" Assiniboin. They found Assiniboin burials on scaffolds and saw other signs of the tribe, but they met no one.

Along the hot, dry section of the Missouri River valley in Montana, we stopped at the Fort Peck Reservation. I looked up an old friend whom I had met years before, an Assiniboin named Ken Ryan. Ken spoke slowly as he translated into English from the Assiniboin oral tradition. He told us that when Lewis and Clark headed west in 1805, the Assiniboin chief Rosebud gave orders to his people not to speak to the intruders.

Lewis, walking along the shore of the river, saw the chief camped nearby and wanted to meet with him. But Rosebud quickly grabbed a long tepee pole and kept Lewis at pole's length as the captain tried to approach. Ken said, "You don't find that information in the journals, do you?"

When we left the reservation, following the Missouri westward, we saw white pelicans, mule deer, and pronghorn antelope. The air was filled with the smell of dry earth and sage. We were now heading into some of the most remote territory in the lower forty-eight states.

*A rainbow crowns the Bears Paw Mountains.*

The explorers kept straining to see the Rockies as they moved through this hot, dry country. For hundreds of miles, the Missouri River had eroded the land like a mammoth ditch. One day, Lewis climbed out of the river bottom and spotted snowcapped mountains. He was overjoyed, but in fact these were not the Rockies. He had spotted the Bears Paw Mountains, a small range that rises dramatically out of the high plains east of the Rockies.

When Suzanna first spotted the Bears Paw Mountains, she pointed to a full rainbow in the sky that covered them like a magic hat. We stopped along the road to pet some horses and watch mule deer bounding through the sage.

*We slept in a cabin near the Missouri River.*

*Old cairns: Years ago people piled rocks to indicate north, south, east, and west.*

## The Wild and Scenic Missouri River

We reached Virgelle, Montana, a one-store town on the Missouri River. People come here to take canoe trips through the White Cliffs and Missouri Breaks, a 149-mile stretch of the Missouri that has been designated a Wild and Scenic River.

We slept in a cabin with no electricity, two rooms, a big old wood cookstove, and kerosene lanterns. It was like living on a farmstead a hundred years ago. Outside was a lovely view of the gentle cliffs, scoured by the great river for thousands of years.

In the morning, Walker and I hiked up onto the plateau above the river and found old cairns, which are piles of rocks used to mark directions. The newer piles could have been made by ranchers clearing the land, but the older ones with the sage growing out of them were probably Native American markers from a long, long time ago. We felt as if we were walking in a sacred place, so we took care not to alter or disturb the cairns.

Later in the morning, we all rode horses for a few hours along the river. At one point, Walker jumped off his horse, reached down, and picked up the pelvis of a dead cow, exclaiming, "Look, Dad, look!" The bones were as big as he was.

## Powwow

That night we drove into the Bears Paw Mountains to a powwow. Tribes from across the Great Plains, from Canada, from Fort Peck and Fort Berthold reservations —Assiniboin, Hidatsa, Cree, Chippewa, Sioux, and more—had come to the Rocky Boy's Reservation to dance, sing, and drum.

At seven-thirty, with a storm approaching, Indians and non-Indians sat around a dance ring, waiting for the Grand Entry that marked the beginning of the all-night affair. When the finely dressed dancers came out, the women formed lines around the circle, and the men, some old and some as young as three or four, danced toward the middle. The haunting beat of the drums and the piercing cries of the dance songs entranced us all.

*Powwow at Rocky Boy's Reservation*

## Tepee Rings

The next morning, in an old pickup truck, Clara Alderice, whose family owns a ten-thousand-acre ranch, drove us way out along the land above the Missouri. We passed over some of the original prairie grass, never cultivated or plowed by modern farmers. We also found the most perfect tepee rings I'd ever seen. Smooth, round stones were laid out in a circle and had been used to hold down the tepees of the Plains Indians for maybe hundreds of years. Perhaps these very rings had been made by the Hidatsa on their way to capture horses and raid the Shoshone.

In the distance, a mother antelope and her twins bounded over the pastel green of the prairie like phantom streaks of light.

When we stopped at some sand dunes, we saw broken arrowheads and fragments of flint lying on the ground. Many native people believe even these tiny chips of flint are part of their cultural heritage and therefore should not be tampered with by anyone.

## Eagle Creek and the White Cliffs

Later that afternoon, local rancher Gary Darlington dropped us off with our canoe in the heart of the White Cliffs. Here at Eagle Creek, across from Labarge Rock, we set up camp. On May 31, 1805, a year after they began their trip, and two months away from Fort

*Tepee rings: Long ago these stones held the bottom edges of tepees in place.*

*An Assiniboin camp photographed in 1908*

Mandan, Sacagawea, her husband and son, the captains, and the rest of the corps had probably slept right where we put our tent.

It was here that Lewis wrote, "The hills and river cliffs which we passed today exhibit a most romantic appearance." For us, too, the cliffs blazed brilliant white in the late afternoon sun. I read aloud from Lewis's journal, "As we passed on, it seemed as if those scenes of visionary enchantment would never have an end."

Suzanna and Walker, however, were more interested in swimming than history. On their backs and stomachs, they floated down the swiftly flowing little riffles of Eagle Creek. Recent rain had brought the water level up, so it was a thrill to get swooped over the rocks and to clutch at the long grass on the banks.

We hopped into the canoe and floated out into the powerful Missouri River, feeling the great current sweep us along the overhanging cliffs of Labarge Rock. We gained new respect for the corps, aware that they had dragged, sailed, poled, and paddled their boats against this current for thousands of miles.

What light the cliff gave off! High up on the cliff an eagle returned to its nest. Beneath the massive stone face, white pelicans skimmed along the water.

*Swimming in Eagle Creek that feeds into the Missouri River*

*Labarge Rock, shining under the summer sun*

*Ancient petroglyphs*

We pulled the canoe onto the sandy shore and walked up to some ancient petroglyphs. Two figures of primitive-looking horses had been carved into the white sandstone perhaps hundreds of years ago. As a storm approached, we made a fire and ate dinner. Like the Plains Indians, we fed our fire with sage and dung (from cattle, not buffalo), filling the air with an exotic scent. As the wind picked up from the west, it grew dark and stormy. There was much left to explore, but the rain was coming soon, so we threw everything inside the tent and dove into our sleeping bags. Through the long night, the wind flapped the tent around like a huge plastic bag.

*Camping near the Missouri River, where Sacagawea and the corps camped on May 31, 1805*

## Great Falls of the Missouri

The next day, we drove to the Great Falls of the Missouri. In the van we read that Sacagawea had fallen deathly ill with fever before she reached the Great Falls. Lewis and Clark had grown fond of Sacagawea, and they worried greatly about the state of her health. Lewis also knew that if she died, without a Shoshone speaker among them, their chances of forming friendly relations with the Shoshone might be jeopardized, and the expedition could possibly be doomed if they could not secure Shoshone horses for the journey over the mountains.

Lewis made Sacagawea drink sulfur water, which seemed to revive her. Fortunately, in time she recovered. The nearly 20-mile portage around the Great Falls of the Missouri, which is really a series of five different waterfalls, took the corps a month of hard labor. But now the expedition was in full sight of the Rockies!

When the corps left the Great Falls behind them, they also left the bison and the Great Plains behind, and for the first time they entered mountain terrain.

*Today's dam on top of the Great Falls of the Missouri*

# Part Two

## Over the Continental Divide

Much of the route the corps took through the Rockies has changed little in the last two hundred years. We were excited to see this wild country. We paddled the Gates of the Mountains, a narrow gorge with cliffs rising a thousand feet above the river. Here, as the corps climbed higher into the Rockies, the captains kept hoping to find the Shoshone. But like the Assiniboin down on the plains, the Shoshone mostly stayed out of sight.

At Three Forks, Montana, three small rivers come together to form what Lewis and Clark described as the beginning of the Missouri River proper. Here we launched our canoe where the Jefferson and Madison Rivers meet, near the very spot where it is thought that Sacagawea was captured by the Hidatsa raiding party. We paddled the swift current of the Missouri headwaters. Through the clear water, the small pebbles on the bottom shone like colored eggs.

### The Jefferson to the Beaverhead

It was raining as we headed up the Jefferson by car to an even smaller stream called the Beaverhead. Here Sacagawea had spotted a rock formation that her people called the Beaver's Head. She told Lewis that now the corps was not far from where her people usually crossed

*Bitterroot Mountains*

the Bitterroot Mountains to the rivers that flowed westward. The Beaverhead River today is one of the great fishing spots in the West, with as many as 2,500 trout living in every mile of water. We saw drift boats, rafts, and sport fishermen.

As the summer of 1805 drew to a close, the corps was still desperately looking for the Shoshone.

*Rock formation that early Native Americans called the Beaver's Head*

*Paddling the
Clark Canyon Reservoir*

## Camp Fortunate

Later in the day, we reached the Clark Canyon Dam and Reservoir. Walker got out of the van, saw the big lake, and asked, "Dad, is this the Pacific Ocean?"

The big blue reservoir, sitting like a small sea in the hot, dry land, now covers the area Lewis and Clark called Camp Fortunate. Lewis got here first. Clark followed, dragging the boats and supplies up the shallow Beaverhead. Lewis left a note for Clark and headed west on foot. He climbed up the Lemhi Pass. He looked out at the snowcapped Bitterroot Mountains and realized for the first time just how formidable the Rockies were. Now he was sure he would need horses to travel overland. From the pass, Lewis descended toward the west and became the first known white man to cross the northern section of the Continental Divide in the present-day United States. The Shoshone, the Nez Perce, the Blackfeet, the Salish, the Assiniboin, and the Hidatsa had been traveling across the Divide for hundreds, probably thousands, of years to hunt and trade.

After leaving the pass, Lewis reached a Shoshone village. He convinced Chief Cameahwait to return 40 miles

25

*The beautiful Lemhi Pass*

*Lewis and Clark meet Native Americans in what is now Montana. Sacagawea and her son are sitting in the grass.*

to the area that would later be named Camp Fortunate, where Clark was supposed to join them. But Clark was late, and when Lewis saw that Clark and his group, including Sacagawea and Charbonneau, hadn't gotten there yet, he was worried the Shoshone might leave, taking with them the possibility of securing any horses.

When Clark finally approached the camp, Sacagawea began to dance, jump, and shout because she recognized her own people.

Reunited, Lewis and Clark smoked a pipe of friendship with Chief Cameahwait. Sacagawea saw that the chief was her very own brother. She ran to him, threw her blanket over him, and cried. Then she sat down and began to translate, often breaking into tears. Translations were not simple. Since she spoke no English, Sacagawea translated her brother's words into Hidatsa. Charbonneau translated the Hidatsa into French, and François Labiche, a member of the corps who often acted as a French translator, translated from the French into English.

Negotiations for horses and the transmitting of basic information took some time. There may have been mistakes in the conveyance of ideas and intentions.

Because Clark had finally arrived and the Shoshone had not left early, the corps named this place Camp Fortunate. They stayed for a week. Lewis and Clark told the chief that he and his people were now under the protection of the U.S. government. They said they had come to find a trade route. The chief drew diagrams of the western rivers for Clark, and he agreed to help the corps, perhaps because Lewis promised a supply of guns. Lewis's men had noticed there were only three or four rifles in the whole Shoshone village.

We camped at Clark Canyon, where Walker found an eagle feather. Since eagle feathers are used for Native American ceremonies and dances, it was illegal to take it with us. So we left it lying on the shore. We considered this place our own Camp Fortunate. Family tensions had been running high after many days of traveling, but now we had a chance to rest and laugh. We played hot potato, and our spirits turned upward.

## Lemhi Pass, August 12, 1805

We packed the van and headed up into the Lemhi Pass. When we reached the top, we had to put on sweaters. The wind was bringing a freezing cloud of rain from the west.

Today was August 12. What a coincidence! Our little corps had reached the Lemhi Pass on the same date Lewis first crossed it nearly two hundred years before us—on August 12, 1805.

Along the ridge, a wooden fence marks the border between Montana and Idaho. This is also the ridge that marks the Continental Divide itself, where the water on the western slope flows to the Pacific and the water on the eastern side goes toward the Atlantic.

*We stood over a small stream in the Lemhi Pass that Meriwether Lewis mistakenly thought was the source of the Missouri River.*

*This fence marks the the Continental Divide, as well as the border between Montana and Idaho.*

# Part Three

## Downhill to the Pacific

We now descended toward the Pacific Ocean, and our journey took on a different feel altogether. We followed rivers like the little Lemhi, the Salmon, the Bitterroot, the Lochsa, the Clearwater, the Snake, and finally the Columbia, all of which were racing to the western sea.

After their stay at Camp Fortunate, Sacagawea and the other members of the expedition crossed the Lemhi Pass to the village of Sacagawea's brother, located in the Lemhi Valley. Clark meanwhile took a few men north to scout the Salmon River to see if it would be possible to reach the Columbia River and the Pacific Ocean by going down the Salmon.

Near the tiny town of Tendoy, Idaho, we passed the site of the long-ago-abandoned Shoshone village on the peaceful Lemhi River where Sacagawea most probably had been born. Cottonwoods lined the brook. We could imagine Lewis's delight when he reached the land of the Shoshone where spotted horses grazed in the valley.

In his journal, corps member Patrick Gass described a Shoshone village: "There are about 25 lodges made of willow bushes. They are the poorest and most miserable nation I ever beheld: having scarcely anything to subsist on, except berries and a few fish. . . . They have a great many fine horses, and nothing more; and on account of these [the horses] they are much harassed by other nations."

*A Shoshone from the Fort Hall Reservation dancing in the Lemhi Valley*

Clark later stopped at a village where the Shoshone had placed a fish weir, a kind of fishnet or fence, across the Lemhi River. Broiled and dried salmon and dried chokecherries were generously given to the corps. Clark recorded how mild the Shoshone disposition was and how sincere their friendship. He also admired the fact that the women shared equally with men in conversations.

Today the Lemhi Valley has one of the largest populations of Rocky Mountain elk in the world. Cougar come down into the valley, and wolves howl from nearby mountains. One evening in the rustic town of Salmon, Idaho, a rainbow thick and bright with color popped out of the sky after a sudden summer rain.

## Shoshone

In Salmon, we watched a group of Shoshone perform some of their traditional dances. A young woman played tunes on her flute as Suzanna stood transfixed by the music. The men, arrayed in eagle feathers, danced expressively while the women made minute, tight steps, lovely in their restraint. But the ceremony seemed sad, too, because for many years the Lemhi Shoshone have not lived in their homeland, the valley of Sacagawea. In 1907, they were moved south to the Fort Hall Reservation, on a march, according to accounts at the time, punctuated by tears and wails. The Lemhi Shoshone are trying to return to their homeland, but it is difficult to find available land, and there is much local opposition.

On August 30, 1805, the Corps of Discovery left the Shoshone and the Lemhi Valley. Sacagawea said good-bye to her people. We have no record in the journals of what that parting was like. Perhaps she wished to stay with her tribe, or, because the Shoshone were so hungry, she might have wanted to keep going with the corps. Nevertheless, she was a married woman, so her responsibility lay with her family.

Before leaving Salmon, we drove along the Salmon River. The white water here is so dangerous, the Salmon is also called "The River of No Return." Clark reported that it was almost one continuous rapid and that passage "with canoes is entirely impossible."

So the expedition had to buy twenty-nine pack horses from the Shoshone and go 110 miles north across the mountains on an Indian trail. Old Toby, a Shoshone man, and his son led the expedition through the Bitterroots. By September 2, it had snowed. Winter had arrived in the mountains!

## Lost Trail Pass

The expedition spent a few grueling days climbing over what is known today as Lost Trail Pass. The ground was covered with snow on September 4, 1805. The corps met a party of the Flathead, or Salish, people. Clark wrote in his journal that there were "33 lodges,

*Women wearing ceremonial dress dancing with delicate steps*

about 80 men, 400 total, and at least 500 horses. Those people received us friendly, threw white robes over our shoulders and smoked in the pipes of peace." The expedition camped with these generous people. Like the Shoshone, the Salish shared what they had with the corps and sold more horses.

Where the expedition camped with the Salish, our little family corps of discovery also camped beside the shallow and lovely Bitterroot River. Walker fished the stream while Melissa and Suzanna picked large wild serviceberries, which tasted like sour blueberries.

*Lochsa River*

## Nez Perce Country

Sacagawea and the corps were dangerously low on food as they crossed over Lolo Pass into Nez Perce country. The Lolo, called "Khusahna Ishkt," or Buffalo Trail, by the Nez Perce, had linked the Columbia River tribes and Northern Plains Indians for hundreds, maybe thousands, of years.

The expedition now faced one of the worst portions of the whole journey. For eleven days it rained and snowed. Game was scarce. Horses stumbled and fell over cliffs. Lightning and hail beset the little group of adventurers, who were so hungry that at one point they killed and ate a colt.

The Nez Perce might easily have wiped out the expedition as it approached their villages west of the mountains, but fortunately they chose not to attack.

As we drove upward into the clouds and the chilly air of the pass, it was hard to imagine Sacagawea with a baby in the harsh conditions that the corps faced in the autumn of 1805. We followed the rapids of the Lochsa River down to the Clearwater River. Here the explorers made five dugout canoes from ponderosa pines for the trip down the Snake and Columbia Rivers.

The Lochsa was the most beautiful white-water river of all the rivers we'd seen so far. Here in the wildest part of Idaho live moose, elk, black bear, wolf, and cougar.

Along the Lochsa we stopped to hike a mile into

natural hot springs, where hot mineral water rises to the surface from deep in the earth and flows down to the cold river, creating steam. There are many hot springs throughout this part of the mountains. High above us, at Lolo Hot Springs, the corps had stopped to rest before pushing over the pass.

## The Heart of the Monster

Like so many other native tribes the corps met along its journey, the Nez Perce greeted the expedition with curiosity and generosity. For two weeks the Corps of Discovery built canoes and rested below the mountains in the Clearwater Valley, near present-day Orofino, recouping, eating salmon and a dried root called camas, which the tribe was preparing for winter storage.

Entrusting their horses to the Nez Perce and accompanied now by three Nez Perce men, the corps left for the sea on October 7, 1805, hoping to be on their way home the next spring. The expedition faced many dangerous rapids on the Clearwater and more on the Snake. Two boats sank, and repairs had to be made.

Along the Snake River, they met other tribes and traded goods for dogs, which they ate. Lewis liked dog meat, but Clark did not. Tribes along the rivers of the Northwest began to call the corps Dog Eaters.

On October 13, Clark wrote in his journal how beneficial it was to have Sacagawea along. "The wife of Charbonneau our interpreter we find reconciles all the

*Resting in natural hot springs*

Indians, as to our friendly intentions. A woman with a party of men is a token of peace."

In Kamiah, Idaho, I talked with Allen Slickpoo, who practices the traditional ways of the tribe and who still speaks the language of the Nez Perce. He told me he was passing along these traditions to his children.

Allen said his people remember Lewis and Clark in conjunction with the missionaries who came a few decades after the expedition. Much of the Nez Perce culture was taken away from the tribe by the missionaries, he said, and the effects of those early missionaries can be seen today.

Slickpoo did not sound bitter, but his message was strong: Lewis and Clark had brought death to the Nez

*The Nez Perce call this mound "The Heart of the Monster."*

Perce way of life. What he meant was not so much that the Corps of Discovery itself had brought destruction, but rather that the corps was the front end of a huge invasion of outsiders that would soon follow, bringing devastating changes to the traditional ways of native life.

In Kamiah, our family slept across from a legendary mound, a volcanic outcropping the Nez Perce call the "Heart of the Monster." According to tribal legend, it was here that Coyote slew the monster and carved him up. As he tossed pieces of the monster to various parts of the Pacific Northwest, the animals and tribes of the world were created. Where the monster's feet fell, for example, the Blackfeet people originated. But the monster's heart was not scattered as was the rest of his body. The heart simply fell to the ground in this very place. And Coyote watered the ground and up sprang the "Nee-MEE-Poo," or "The People" as the Nez Perce call themselves. This unassuming rock outcropping was the heart of the Nez Perce nation, and we considered it a blessing to have slept near such a sacred place.

## Panning for Gold

We met a prospector who told us where to pan for gold on the Clearwater River near Lewiston, Idaho. We bought pans and went to the riverside on a perfect sunny day. In the afternoon glare, we swirled the river muck around until little yellow flakes showed in our pans. Suzanna and Walker put their gold into small glass vials.

*Panning for gold*

This was flood gold that had washed down from the mountains thousands of years ago. The tiny, thin flakes were not worth much in dollars, but they were worth a great deal in the richness of the experience.

Downriver from Lewiston, the Clearwater opened into the Snake River, and the air turned even hotter. The land was as brown and dry as a desert. Along the Snake, we saw our first tugboats and real industry. We were getting closer to the sea.

When the corps arrived at the confluence of the Snake and Columbia Rivers on October 16, 1805, they were greeted by hundreds of Wanapum and Yakima Indians. Salmon were running in the river. The corps mended their clothes, updated their journals, and prepared to push on to the Pacific.

*Camping in the Pacific Northwest*

## Columbia River

Sacagawea and her child faced more rapids and waterfalls on the Columbia. The expedition met other tribes catching salmon and drying fillets on fish racks along shore. The Nez Perce guides returned to their homeland, and the corps began to see evidence of sea trade among the peoples of the Columbia River. These people had been visited for years by British and Yankee ships sailing along the coast.

Then on November 7, 1805, Clark wrote, "Ocean in view. O. The Joy." Actually, when Clark wrote this, he may have been looking at the wide mouth of the great rolling Columbia River, not the sea itself. But he was close. He was standing on the north shore of the river, just east and opposite of present-day Astoria, Oregon. Near the sea at last, the group's exuberance was tempered by days of hunger, darkness, and dreariness. The rain, wind, fog, and gloom became daily trials to overcome.

Our own little corps of discovery was weary from nearly a month of travel in the modern dugout of our Chevy van. We were happy to reach the sea, but our joy was also tempered by fatigue and by the fog rolling in from the Pacific. The giant cedars, spruce, and hemlock of the Pacific Northwest looked like fantastic animals with coats of moss on every branch and trunk.

*The Columbia River*

Lewis and Clark with Sacagawea and
Charbonneau on the Columbia River

# Part Four

## Fort Clatsop

Like Lewis and Clark, we camped in the rain forest. We set up our tent at Fort Stevens State Park, a few miles from where the expedition spent the winter of 1805–1806. Once again, we noticed how engaged our senses were when we spent a night camping instead of staying at a motel. The outdoors put us all in better spirits. Collecting wood, preparing dinner, being active—this saved us.

Fort Clatsop is a small, square-shaped structure. It has been meticulously reconstructed from a copy of Clark's floor plan, which he drew in his journal. As at Mandan, the fort was named after the local tribe, the Clatsops. It seemed a neat and cozy place, but we could not imagine being stuck here month after month in bad weather without going a little crazy.

To get away from the pounding weather of the sea, the explorers had built their fort seven miles inland from the Pacific. Nearby, Clark carved these words into a big fir tree: "Capt William Clark December 3rd 1805. By Land. U. States in 1804 & 1805." But that carving disappeared long ago.

The day we arrived at Fort Clatsop, it was drizzling. Walker and Suzanna lay down on bunk beds covered in animal hides. A fire smoldered in the fireplace of the

*Bunks in Fort Clatsop*

captains' quarters, right next to the little room where Charbonneau, Sacagawea, and Jean Baptiste slept. We could picture Lewis and Clark sitting here by the fire, spending those cold and dreary months rewriting their journals and perfecting their maps.

On January 6, 1806, Clark set out with a small group to get blubber from a beached whale near the ocean. Sacagawea said she wanted to go along to the "great waters" she had come so far to see, so Clark took her with him. But when they got to the hundred-foot-long whale, they found it had already been stripped clean by the Tillamook people who lived nearby.

In one hundred and six days at the fort, it rained all but twelve, and only six days were sunny. Sacagawea must have longed for the sunlight of the plains.

Finally, on March 23, 1806, the group headed back the way they had come. Perhaps it would have been better to delay their journey until April, but they were eager to leave the Pacific Ocean and get home.

Other adventures and setbacks awaited them on the return journey. Snows beset them in the Rockies, and they had to turn back once. Sacagawea continued to provide a number of important services, including those of interpreter, trader, food gatherer, and geographer.

Returning to present-day Montana, the party split up. Clark's group, including Sacagawea, returned to Camp Fortunate and then headed down the Yellowstone River. Clark carved his name and the date in a sandstone tower along the Yellowstone. It survives to this day, the only physical evidence of the expedition. Lewis's group went north to explore the Marias River. A few months later, both groups were reunited and managed to reach the Mandan and Hidatsa villages.

Unfortunately, they found Fort Mandan had been destroyed by a prairie fire. They stayed three days, and on August 17, 1806, the captains said good-bye to Sacagawea and her family. The Corps of Discovery then continued down the Missouri to St. Louis, successfully completing one of the greatest fact-finding expeditions of all time.

*Fort Clatsop, reconstructed*

*Lowering the flag at sunset*

It was September 1806, two years and four months after setting out, and the explorers were greeted as heroes. Three years later, Clark would meet Sacagawea and Charbonneau again. They came to St. Louis to place Jean Baptiste under Clark's guardianship. During the two-year journey to the Pacific Ocean and back, Clark had grown much attached to Jean Baptiste and now promised to educate the child. Maybe Sacagawea thought her son would have a better life with Clark, but I couldn't help wondering how difficult giving up her son must have been for the young Shoshone woman, especially after forming such a unique bond with Jean Baptiste on their amazing trek to the Pacific and back.

Before we left Fort Clatsop, one of the national park rangers asked Suzanna and Walker if they would help her take down the flag. It seemed fitting at the end of our journey for them to put on replicas of the two dress coats Captains Lewis and Clark wore when meeting chiefs and conducting affairs of state. The coats, although much too big for my children, looked stately in that raw, gray drizzle of Fort Clatsop.

The flag was a replica of the one the corps had flown on the Pacific coast before they set out on their return voyage. It had fifteen stars and stripes. There were actually seventeen states in 1804, but this was the official flag until 1820. Then more stars were added to represent twenty states. The young nation was growing quickly.

The flag came down slowly. Suzanna helped fold it, and our trip was done.

*The Pacific Ocean: Our journey's end*

Just one last photo to take, I told the kids, and I assembled the family on the beach of the great ocean. The sea was gray, the sky was gray, but I felt anything but gray. Walker and Suzanna had grown sick of my taking photos of our trip. When I tried to line them up on the beach, they fled from my cameras until a seal from under a jetty suddenly started to bark. Walker and the seal barked at each other. Then Walker found a dead crab among the big black beach boulders, and he lifted it up with glee. Offshore, surfers in wet suits cruised the cold, gray expanse for good waves. And for an hour or so we stood at the edge of the sea, wondering at our good fortune and letting the story of Sacagawea and the Corps of Discovery filter down through the years and into our hearts.

### Who was Sacagawea?

Sacagawea was not so much a guide to the expedition as perhaps a guardian for this great journey of discovery. President Jefferson had had the vision to send the Corps of Discovery out into the new territories of the United States and beyond. Lewis and Clark and their men had realized Jefferson's vision, but most probably they could not have succeeded without Sacagawea, who helped secure horses to get over the Rockies before the winter came, helped find roots and plants to eat, and acted as a symbol of friendship for this band of strangers traveling in Indian lands.

Most historians agree that Sacagawea was captured by a Hidatsa raiding party when she was ten or eleven years old. The young Shoshone girl was brought back to the Knife River to be raised in a Hidatsa village. But at the Fort Berthold Reservation, while having lunch with a group of Hidatsa, we had learned different versions of her story. In the oral tradition of the tribe, passed down from generation to generation, some say Sacagawea was Hidatsa. This tradition holds that Sacagawea made a trip to the Rockies before Lewis and Clark arrived and therefore was knowledgeable about the Shoshone but was not Shoshone herself. Another version says she had been captured by the Shoshone and then walked back home with ten pairs of moccasins for the 1,000-mile-long journey along the Missouri River, changing footwear as the moccasins

*Many Shoshone believe that Sacagawea is buried here, on the Wind River Reservation in Wyoming.*

wore out. Whatever the truth is, the Hidatsa say that part of the mystery of her identity was created by the interpreters for Lewis and Clark, who got many pieces of information wrong when they translated from one language to another.

Sacagawea's death remains something of an enigma, too. Many historians say she died a few years after the expedition in what is now South Dakota. Some believe, however, that she lived to be an old woman, much revered throughout the West, and is now buried with her Shoshone ancestors.

Some say that Sacagawea carried a medallion from the president of the United States, along with documents explaining who she was and what she had accomplished; that she traveled on stagecoaches for free; that she helped many Indian people and was much respected until the day she died.

One oral tradition in the Northwest says that Sacagawea traveled as far north as Alaska with former members of the Canadian fur trading companies, perhaps as a guide.

Because we do not know more than what little is written about her in the journals and what remains of her story in the oral traditions of the Shoshone, the Assiniboin, the Hidatsa, and other tribes, Sacagawea, Bird Woman, will remain ever a mystery—a wonderful example of fortitude to give us all heart in our daily adventures.

Following the trail of Sacagawea taught our family many lessons about courage, stamina, and discovery. Mostly we felt we'd been given a gift by seeing some of the sights she had witnessed all those many years ago.

## Notes

■ There are various spellings and pronounciations of Sacagawea's name. Lewis and Clark spelled it seventeen different ways in their journals. Many people call her Sacajawea, and some claim this spelling comes from the Shoshone language. But in Hidatsa, her name is pronounced "Sah-KAH-gah-wee-ah," and is sometimes spelled "Sakakawea." *Sakaka* means "bird" in the Hidatsa language, and *wea* means "woman."

■ Sacagawea's placement within the overall Shoshone tribe is complex. Most probably she was born in the Lemhi Valley of east-central Idaho. She was a member of the Agaiduka, or Lemhi, Shoshone tribe (Northern Shoshone). The name *Lemhi* was given to this group of Shoshone by early settlers in the area, and many today prefer the term *Agaiduka* instead of Lemhi. The Agaiduka do not consider themselves members of the Shoshone-Bannock, or Sho-Ban, people of Fort Hall, which is located a few hundred miles south of the Lemhi Valley. Nor do they consider themselves members of the Wind River Shoshone (Eastern Shoshone) of Wyoming.

■ The Lewis and Clark National Historic Trail and many of the sites connected to Sacagawea are important parts of the cultural landscape. Some sites may be sacred to certain tribes. It is crucial, therefore, that all sites are respected by those who travel on the trail of Sacagawea. Such artifacts as cairns, petroglyphs, pictographs, tepee rings, stone tools, and so on that are found at these sites should not be picked up, altered, or defaced in any way.

Published by Caroline House
Boyds Mills Press, Inc.
A Highlights Company
815 Church Street
Honesdale, Pennsylvania 18431
Printed in China

U.S. Cataloging-in-Publication Data
   (Library of Congress Standards)

Lourie, Peter.
   On the trail of Sacagawea / written and photographed by Peter
Lourie. —1st edition.
[48]p. : col. Ill. (maps) ;   cm.
Summary: A present-day journey that follows Sacagawea's trail, from Fort
Mandan in North Dakota to Fort Clatsop in Oregon.
ISBN 1-56397-840-7
1. Sacagawea, 1786–1884.  2. Lewis and Clark Expedition, 1804–1806.  I.Title.
978. 004/9745  21  2001   AC   CIP
00-102351


First edition, 2001
The text of this book is set in 13-point Berkeley Book.

10 9 8 7 6 5 4 3 2 1

The author wishes to thank the following individuals for their help in the creation of this book: Marilyn Hudson, administrator, Three Affiliated Tribes Museum and a member of the Three Affiliated Tribes of the Fort Berthold Reservation (Mandan, Hidatsa, and Arikara); Dr. Kenneth Ryan, project coordinator for the Administration for Native Americans (ANA), Washington, D.C.; Steven Gregory Lee, president, Idaho Chapter of the Lewis and Clark Trail Heritage Foundation; Sally Freeman, Fort Clatsop National Memorial; Pat Williams, Fort Clatsop National Memorial; Barb Kubik, historian, Washington State Chapter, Lewis and Clark Trail Heritage Foundation.

Additional photographs courtesy of Denver Public Library, Western History Department: p. 9 (*Buffalo and Elk on the Upper Missouri* by Karl Bodmer), p. 38 (*Lewis and Clark on the Columbia* by Frederic Remington), p. 45 (from a painting by Edgar S. Paxon), p. 46 (Sacagawea's grave);  Library of Congress: pp. 13, 14, 18, back jacket; National Park Service: p. 12; Montana Historical Society: p. 26 (*Lewis and Clark Meeting Indians at Ross' Hole* by Charles M. Russell); Oregon State Capitol Building, Oregon State Archives: jacket; State Historical Society of North Dakota: p. 7; Three Forks Area Historical Society and Headwaters Heritage Museum, Three Forks, Montana: p. 22.

# WORLD'S CUTEST HORSES AND PONIES in 3D

Written by Lisa Regan • Design by Debbie Fisher
Developed & Published by Red Bird Publishing Ltd., U.K.
Original 3D special effects developed by
Red Bird Publishing Ltd., U.K.

This edition published by Scholastic Inc., 557 Broadway, New York,
NY 10012, by arrangement with Red Bird Publishing Ltd.

Distributed by Scholastic Canada Ltd, Markham, Ontario
ISBN: 978-0-545-55718-4

10 9 8 7 6 5 4 3 2 1

Printed in Shenzhen, China

# WORLD'S CUTEST HORSES AND PONIES in 3D

Horses and ponies have been a part of people's lives for thousands of years. Today, they are beloved pets, kept for their talents as sports horses, or for the hard work they do on farms. Show horses live a life of luxury, while working horses are prized for their strength, power, and stamina.

# CONTENTS

There are many different breeds of horses and ponies. They are all related to other equines (the name for the horse family), such as zebras and donkeys. Their early ancestors lived up to 55 million years ago and had toes instead of hooves.

# RED AND BLACK

Horses can be a whole range of colors, but horse breeders divide them into two main groups with special names for the different shades. Red horses include bay, chestnut, and all the brown and cream variations. Black horses are less common. A horse with black skin will often have dark and white hairs making it look gray. Horses that look white are classified as grays!

## APPALOOSA

Appaloosa is a breed of horse that has a distinctive spotted pattern like a leopard. They usually have stripes on their hooves and a white ring around the edge of their eye.

## DAPPLED GRAY

Certain horses start life as one color and then turn gray, often when they lose their foal coat. Some, like this one, pass through a dapple stage with dark rings which have pale centers.

## PINTO

The white and colored patches on these animals make them pintos. They are sometimes known as piebald (black and white) or skewbald (any other color).

## CHESTNUT
These horses are reddish brown. They can be very dark (described as liver colored) or pale, but the middle shade of sorrel is the most common for a chestnut.

## PALOMINO
Palominos are a beautiful golden color, sometimes darker, with a distinctive white mane and tail.

## BUCKSKIN AND BLACK
Buckskin horses are a creamy-colored variety of bay. Black horses can fade to a brown shade in the summer sun.

**DID YOU KNOW?**
A foal is often a much paler color than it will become when it gets older.

## COLOR CODED

Many horse lovers think that sorrel horses are flightier than other colors of horse, and that black horses tend to be slow-natured and sleepy. Sorrel and chestnut horses make up over a third of registered American Quarter horses, while black ones are less than 5 percent.

# MAKING THEIR MARK

Not all horses and ponies are a single color all over. Many of them get their character (and cute factor!) from markings that make them look different. Horse breeders have special names for the white markings on a horse's face and legs.

## PONY PORTRAIT
This horse has face markings that almost join together. It has a star and stripe on its forehead, a blaze, and snip on its muzzle.

## BAY HORSES
Reddish-brown horses, known as bay horses, always have a black mane, tail, and legs. The edges of the ears are also black.

## GROWING UP
A horse's markings are there when it is born. They don't change as the horse grows older. This foal will have the same "bald face" marking when it grows up.

## DID YOU KNOW?

Horses can get sunburned skin, especially on the pinky skin under white markings.

## LEG WEAR

Leg markings are stockings or socks. Socks stop below the knee. A small white mark around the hoof is called a coronet.

## UNDERCOAT

The skin underneath white hair is usually pink.

## WHO ARE YOU?

These horses are the same color but have different markings so you can tell them apart. Purebred horse markings are recorded to help identify them at horse shows.

**STAND OUT FROM THE CROWD**
Bay horses have black "points" as part of their natural color. They can also have individual white markings, like the one on the left, which has a star on its forehead.

Sometimes, when a horse has a marking over its eye, the eye might be blue instead of brown.

# HORSE TALK

Horses lovers may use words that you haven't heard before. Horses have specific names for their colors and markings, as well as their body parts. These are known as the "points" of a horse.

## CONFORMATION
A horse is built to run fast or for long distances. Its body shape is called its "conformation". Horses are bred with the conformation needed to be strong, fast, or have a lot of stamina.

## EYE SEE!
Horses' eyes are on the sides of the head, not the front. This helps them to see things sneaking up from around them, but they have to move their head to see things that are close. They can also see separately with each eye!

Some horse words are based on the Latin word for horse, which is "equus" (say "eck-wus"). For example, horse sports are known as equestrian sports.

## JUST THE JOB
A horse's legs may look thin, but they are strong and powerful. They allow it to stop, start, turn very quickly, and to push off into a graceful jump over an obstacle.

## DID YOU KNOW?
A horse's hooves are actually its toes.

## BODY FACTS
A horse walks on its toes, like cats and dogs, not on its whole foot, like a human. The "withers" are where the neck and back join, below the bottom of the mane.

## FACE FACTS
The hair that grows forward between a horse's ears, like a fringe, is its forelock. Its soft nose is the muzzle, with large nostrils that let it breathe in plenty of air when it is moving quickly. Its nostrils are sometimes called "nares".

## RUNAWAY!

A horse's body is designed to keep it safe in the wild. Horses are prey animals. That means they are possible food for predators hunting for meat. Horses are designed to escape rather than stand and fight. That's why they don't have sharp claws or teeth. They have to be able to run faster than the animal chasing them.

### DID YOU KNOW?

Domesticated horses often wear shoes to protect their hooves. The shoes are usually made of metal and fixed in place by a blacksmith.

# TALL AND SMALL

Horses and ponies are measured in hands. One hand is 4 inches (101.6mm). They are measured from the ground to the withers, where the neck meets the back. The tiniest horses are Falabellas, while breeds like the Shire Horse and Percheron are enormous!

### BIG BELGIAN
One of the largest horse breeds is the Belgian draft horse. The tallest ones stand over 19 hands (76 in., 193 cm) high. They can be seen at state fairs pulling heavy loads because they are very strong.

### SMALL IS BEAUTIFUL
These Shetland ponies are only foals, but even when they are fully grown they won't be more than 11 hands high (44 in., 111.7 cm).

### SUPER SHIRE
Shire horses grow very tall. Males can be more than 17 hands (68 in., 172.7 cm) high. They are easy to recognize because of their height but also by the white feathering on their legs, which can cover their hooves.

## CAN YOU SEE ME?

Shetland ponies may be small, but they are strong for their size. They can carry a rider on their back or be put in harness to pull a small cart or carriage.

## HIDE AND SEEK

The Falabella is a rare breed of horse. They are usually no more than 8 hands (32 in., 81.28 cm) high. Foals are only 1 to 2 ft. (30.5 cm to 61 cm) tall when they are born. Cute!

## RECORD BREAKERS

The record for the world's largest horse is often held by a Percheron. These magnificent creatures are usually black or gray. They are intelligent animals with a lot of strength and energy.

## DID YOU KNOW?

Horses must be measured without shoes to get their correct official height.

17

## SHORT BUT STRONG

Shetland ponies are popular riding ponies as they work well, are gentle, and they don't eat as much as larger horses! They are originally from islands off the chilly coast of Scotland, so they have long coats to keep them warm in winter. Their long forelock and mane protects their eyes, head, and neck in icy conditions.

## DID YOU KNOW?

These cute creatures are so strong they can pull twice their own bodyweight. A large draft horse can pull only half its own weight!

# SPOT THE DIFFERENCE

Many people start to ride on a pony, not a horse. But what is the difference? One easy thing to spot is the height: a pony is less than 14.2 hands (56.8 in., 144.2 cm) high. Ponies also have a different body shape with shorter legs, smaller ears, and a thick, broad body and neck. That's why a miniature horse is a horse not a pony—it has the right proportions for a horse but is very small.

## DID YOU KNOW?

Miniature horses were once bred to be cute pets for kings and queens.

### LONG LEGS
Miniature horses have the same body shape (known as "conformation") as their larger relatives. Their legs are long in proportion to their body. They have a fine, slim head, too.

### EASY RIDER
Ponies are often used to teach children how to ride. Many of them are too small to take an adult rider.

## FULL OF FEED
A pony only eats half the food a horse eats, even if they are the same weight.

## HANDY HELPERS
Miniatures can be trained to assist people with disabilities. They are very good for people with dog allergies or phobias, and live longer than a guide dog, too.

## LONG LIVED
Both horses and ponies can live 25–30 years on average, but many more ponies grow much older than that—some as old as 50 years.

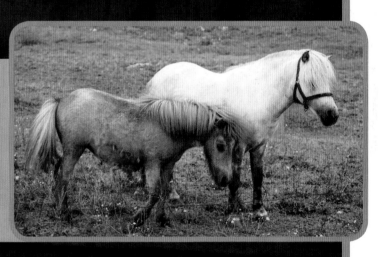

## PONY CLUB
Certain breeds are said to be ponies no matter what their height. These include Welsh ponies, Connemaras, and Quarter ponies, which are all good for learning to ride.

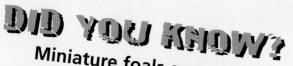

## DID YOU KNOW?

Miniature foals generally measure between 15 and 22 in. (38 and 55.8 cm) at birth. And they are adorable!

## MINI WORKERS

Many miniature horses can be traced back to European ancestors. Some were bred to work in coal mines, pulling carts full of coal in very small spaces. These days, a horse must be less than 38 in. (96.5 cm) tall to be registered as a miniature.

# KEEP IT IN THE FAMILY

In the wild, horses live in herds. A herd will have the right mixture of males and females, and old and young horses. A foal is a baby horse, less than one year old. Grown-up males are called stallions, and adult females are mares.

## MOM-TO-BE
A mare will be pregnant for around 11 months. Human mothers are pregnant for only 9 months.

## BABY NAMES
A colt is a young male (under 4 years old). A female of the same age is a filly.

## RELATIVELY SPEAKING
The mother of a foal is known as the dam, and the father as the sire. Horse breeders like to know about a foal's family history, such as whether its parents were racehorses or working horses.

## DID YOU KNOW?
Foals are much more likely to be born at night.

## BABY LONG LEGS

A foal's legs are nearly as long as an adult's. They are about nine-tenths their fully grown length.

## GIDDY UP!

A foal can stand up less than an hour after it is born, and can trot and canter within hours. It will be able to gallop when it is a day old.

**DID YOU KNOW?**
Horses are naturally preyed on in the wild, so they need to be born quickly and be able to run away soon after birth.

## HORSEY BIRTHDAY

A horse's birthday is always listed as January 1 (August 1 in the southern hemisphere). So a horse born in July, 2013 will still have a birth date of January 1, 2013. Many breeders don't like their foals to come late in the year, as they will have their first birthday only days or weeks after they were born!

# WORKING HORSES

Horses are given all sorts of jobs to do. Their strength makes them really useful for pulling things. Horses can be trained to work with their rider in dangerous situations, like police horses. Racehorses and show horses are worth a lot of money, and are taken care of very well.

## TWO TIDY
The manes of these horses have been neatly braided. This keeps the mane tidy during show events such as jumping and dressage.

## TRUSTY STEEDS
Cowboys in the 19th century relied totally on their horses. They would ride for many miles (kilometers) to round up and transfer cattle. Even today, cowboys still use horses to cover the rough terrain of the Great Plains.

## WAR HORSE

The Lusitano breed of horse originally came from Portugal. It was bred to carry soldiers in war and for bullfighting.

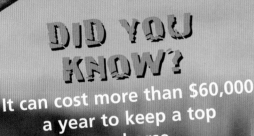

## HARD AT WORK

The Suffolk Punch is still used as a working draft horse. They are always chestnut in color but are becoming a rare breed.

## DON'T LOOK NOW

Horses are easily spooked by things around them. Work horses wear blinders (also called winkers or blinkers) to stop them from getting so scared.

## HORSE POWER

Years ago horses pulled farm machinery, but now that machines have taken over they are more likely to pull carts, carriages, or heavy logs in forest work. They can still be seen in action at shows and on a few small farms.

## HOW MUCH POWER

An engine's power is measured in "horse power"; for example, many Mustang cars have a 210 horsepower engine. James Watt, a Scottish engineer from the 1700s, first used the term to describe the power of an engine compared to the number of draft horses needed to do the same work.

## DID YOU KNOW?

The world's biggest horse museum is in Lexington, Kentucky. The state is famous for its horse activities, especially the Kentucky Derby race which is held every May.

## DID YOU KNOW?

Draft horses like these Belgians were used in wars to move heavy guns, pull carts of injured soldiers, and carry important generals high above the troops.

# WILD HORSES

Horses haven't always lived a cozy life in a stable, or with humans caring for them. They were originally wild animals, well adapted to life on the move, watching out for predators. Their body is built for escape, and their coat is designed to see them through the toughest weather conditions.

## NOT WILD

Most horses, even those that don't belong to anyone, are descended from domesticated breeds. This is why they are not "wild" in the same way as Przewalski's (say "shee-val-skees") horses.

## KEEPING WARM

A horse's coat must keep it warm and dry in harsh weather. Some breeds, like Shetland ponies, have a coat that gets thicker in winter. This keeps out the cold but also stops rain from getting through to the horse's skin. In summer, the extra fur is lost.

## FRINGE BENEFITS

Many horses with descendents from cold climates have a long, shaggy mane and forelock. It is thought that the hair helps to protect the neck and eyes from icy cold winds and low temperatures.

## FREE TO ROAM

Exmoor ponies seem wild, as they wander freely across the moors of southwest England, but all the herds have owners.

## MOUNTAIN PONY

Some breeds of pony are naturally tougher than others for coping with cold weather.

## WILD THINGS

The only true wild horses left are called Przewalski's horses. They live in Asia and are almost extinct.

## STICKING TOGETHER

Przewalski's horses live in herds in Mongolia and China. They are small—about 13 hands (52 in., 15.08 cm) high—and always have a pale body and dark tail and legs. Other countries have herds of part-domesticated horses living in the wild, such as the Brumby of Australia, the Mustang in the USA, and Sorraia horses in Spain and Portugal.

There used to be another breed of wild horse, the Tarpan, but that became extinct in the 1920s.

## DID YOU KNOW?

Wild horses like Przewalski's don't have a forelock of hair tumbling forward.

# ON THE MOVE

The different ways a horse moves are known as "gaits." A wild horse has four natural paces or gaits: walk, trot, canter, and gallop. It is possible for a rider to train their horse to do other paces as well.

### WALKING
Walking is the slowest gait. The horse moves one foot at a time, and keeps three feet on the ground.

### TROTTING
Trotting is the next speed up from walking. In Western riding, a slow trot is called jogging. The horse moves two legs at a time, in diagonal pairs.

## WILD AND FREE

Horses love to run! In the wild, they will gallop along together just for the fun of it.

## DID YOU KNOW?

The fastest horses can reach top speeds of over 50 mph (80 kph).

## QUICK DASH

Horses can gallop very fast, but not for too long. They will begin to tire and slow down after a mile (kilometer) or two. Like other wild animals, this top speed running is for escaping predators.

## CANTER

As the horse gets faster and starts running, it reaches a canter, or lope. It pushes off with one back leg so it always has one foot on the ground. Cantering is nearly as fast as galloping but with a different rhythm.

## GALLOPING

Think of a race horse running its fastest and that's what galloping looks like. All four feet actually leave the ground at the same time. A horse can usually gallop at about 30 mph (48 kph).

Horses cool down after running by sweating. Most animals can't sweat.

**RUNNING AWAY**
Sometimes a herd will run because it is scared. A spooked horse will usually run at a lope or a canter. This allows it to stay running for longer without getting tired.

# MY LITTLE PONY

Horses need lots of care and attention. So owning one is time-consuming. They like regular routine and need to be checked every day to make sure they are healthy. You will need to find time to feed, groom, exercise, and clean up after your horse.

## SADDLE UP

You will need special equipment for your horse. A halter goes over his head so you can lead him or tie him up. Reins help you direct your horse when you're riding. A saddle and stirrups let you sit safely on his back.

## POISONOUS PLANTS

If your horse spends time in a field, you must check that poisonous plants are removed. Some wild flowers and trees are dangerous for a horse to eat. They might be growing in the field, or within reach around the edge. These plants include crab apples, buttercups, poppies, rhododendron, milkweed, foxglove, yew, and ragwort.

## CHANGING SEASONS

A horse that lives in a stable in winter should be gradually introduced to its summer field so that it doesn't eat too much grass all at once—this will make it sick.

## DID YOU KNOW?

Acorns (from oak trees) can be dangerous if your horse eats lots of them.

### EATING GRASS

A horse has a small stomach so it can't eat large amounts all at once. It is best for horses to munch on grass or hay throughout the day. This is called "grazing". Some horses are fed grain but not all of them need it. For example, small ponies and horses that don't get much exercise.

### WHO'S THERE?

Horses need exercise, and the company of other horses, so make sure your horse isn't left alone in a stable all day long.

Skipping out (also called skepping out) is a quick clean up of a stall or paddock to get rid of droppings. Mucking out involves removing all the straw and replacing it with clean bedding.

## TIDY UP

Grooming your horse is an important job. It will keep him clean and comfortable. It's also a good chance to check for cuts, swelling, or other problems, and simply to spend time together. A less pleasant job is "mucking out"—cleaning up horse droppings and dirty straw. Even a field needs to be tilled now and then so weeds and bad grasses don't grow.

# ALL TOGETHER NOW

Horses are social animals that like to be with other horses. They love company so much they will make friends with other farm animals, like goats! Watch horses together and you will see how they nuzzle and groom each other, and "talk" with different noises and actions.

## WET AND WILD

Some horses aren't afraid of water and will cross rivers and streams. Other horses have to be taught to enter water. If they see another horse going in, they are likely to become brave enough to follow.

## GOOD NEIGHBORS

Horses often face each other and "groom" their friend with their teeth. This shows how much they trust and like each other.

## DID YOU KNOW?

Horses can sleep standing up!

## HOW YOU DOIN'?

A group of horses will sometimes put their noses together. Sharing each other's breath like this shows trust and friendship.

## LEADER OF THE PACK

Horses in the wild live in herds. The herd has a leader that chooses where they go, when they travel, who eats and drinks first, and so on. The group protects one another from dangers such as predators and takes care of the young.

## MUZZLE NUZZLE

Smell is important to a horse. Mothers recognize their babies by smell rather than sight.

## DO YOU SPEAK HORSE?

Horses make a "nickering" noise to say hello. They do it to humans that they trust and to other horses they know. Mothers often do it to comfort their foals or to show they are worried (if the foal runs off).

## HAVING A REST

Foals lie down to rest much more often than adults. An adult horse will lock its legs so it can snooze standing up, without falling over. They only need to lie down and sleep every few days. This helps to keep the whole herd safe in the wild.

## HORSE TALK

A horse tells you as much with its "body language" as it does with noises. Its ears can show you whether it is nervous, angry, relaxed, interested, or afraid.

## DID YOU KNOW?

A horse that is flicking its tail is likely to kick out. Stand back!

# ROUNDUP

Horses are fascinating creatures. Whether you want to own one of your own or just like to go horseback riding now and then, you will have a great time around horses and ponies. The more you know about them, the more you will grow to understand them. Here are a few final, curious facts for you...

### HEY, NOSEY!
Horses don't breathe through their mouth like we do. They only breathe through their nose. Their nostrils expand during exercise to take in more air.

### TOUCHY FEELY
Horses can't see directly in front of them because of the shape of their face! They have whiskers, just like cats and dogs, which help the horse to judge when its muzzle is close to an object.

### KEEP SMILING
A horse's teeth never stop growing!

### NOT THE SAME
Many Arab horses have a different number of bones from other breeds.